KLAUS BAUMGART lives with his family in Berlin. The LAURA'S STAR series has had multi-million sales worldwide. It has been broadcast on TV throughout Europe, including in the UK, and the first title, LAURA'S STAR, has been made into a film. Klaus Baumgart was the first German author/illustrator to be shortlisted for the Children's Book Award in 1999 for LAURA'S STAR.

Also available by Klaus Baumgart:

Picture Books
LAURA'S STAR
LAURA'S CHRISTMAS STAR
LAURA'S SECRET

First Readers
LAURA'S STAR AND THE NEW TEACHER
LAURA'S STAR AND THE SLEEPOVER
LAURA'S STAR AND THE SEARCH FOR SANTA

Activity Book
LAURA'S STAR STICKER ACTIVITY BOOK

LITTLE TIGER PRESS
An imprint of Magi Publications
1 The Coda Centre, 189 Munster Road, London SW6 6AW
www.littletigerpress.com

First published in Great Britain 2008
Originally published in Germany 2007
by Baumhaus Verlag, Frankfurt

Text and illustrations copyright © Klaus Baumgart 2007
Translation by Dawn Lacy
English text copyright © Little Tiger Press 2008
Klaus Baumgart has asserted his right to be identified as the author
and illustrator of this work under the Copyright, Designs and Patents Act, 1988

A CIP catalogue record for this book is available from the British Library

Laura's Star

and the Special Pony

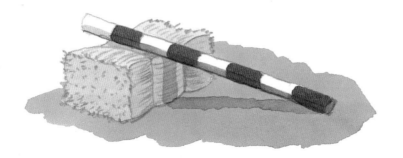

Klaus Baumgart

English text by Fiona Waters

LITTLE TIGER PRESS
London

Laura's Wish

Laura knelt on her bed, looking out of the window. She could see her friend, the star, as it sparkled high in the sky. She sighed deeply and the star twirled around and twinkled down at her.

"Oh Star!" whispered Laura. "I do wish I had my own pony!"

During her school holidays,

Laura had taken riding lessons. It had been great fun and so exciting! It was quite difficult too. Every time the pony had taken a step, Laura found herself slipping from side to side. But the ponies were so friendly and so lovely with their warm, shiny coats and soft, snuffly noses.

Laura was longing to ride again.

The riding stables were next door to Granny and Grandad's house, and the horses grazed in Granny and Grandad's meadow. On Sunday, the day after tomorrow, there was going to be a gymkhana in the meadow.

"We are all going together to watch," Laura told her star. "Except, I don't just want to watch; I want to ride in the gymkhana too!"

But without a pony to ride, Laura wouldn't be able to take part.

She sighed again. "It really isn't so much to wish for! Looking after a pony can't be a lot of trouble, can it? What do you think, Star? Perhaps you could help me persuade Mum and Dad to let me have a pony?"

But when Laura mentioned it to Dad the next morning he wasn't very enthusiastic.

"Laura, it's far too expensive to keep a pony!" he said. "And anyway, where would you keep one here in the city?"

"Our flat is big enough!" insisted Laura.

Tommy, who was sitting at the kitchen table, wrinkled up his nose.

"It certainly can't live in my bedroom!" he said. "Horses smell!"

"They do not!" replied Laura huffily. "Anyway, it would live in my bedroom of course!"

"There aren't any ponies small enough to fit into your bedroom, Laura!" Dad laughed. "Now off you go!" And he sent Laura and Tommy to buy some bread from the baker's shop.

The Pony on the Street Corner

Laura and Tommy walked down to the shops.

"Did Dad give us enough money for cakes as well?" asked Tommy.

"I don't know!" muttered Laura. She was still thinking about her conversation with Dad.

Laura suddenly stopped, her eyes wide open in astonishment. On the

corner of the street was a man,
collecting money in a tin. And next
to the man, there was a pony!

The pony was tiny. The top of
its ears only just reached up to the
man's chest. But it was a real pony,
with four polished hooves, a shiny,
brown coat and a lovely white
mane. In the middle of its forehead
was a little white mark.

The man noticed Laura and Tommy and waved across at them.

"Hello," he said. "Would you like to stroke Polly?" Tommy shook his head, but Laura nodded and reached out her hand.

"Don't, it might bite you!" Tommy whispered to Laura.

"You needn't be afraid! Polly is perfectly friendly!" said the man, smiling at Tommy.

Laura stroked Polly on the nose. And what a soft nose it was! The pony sniffed at Laura's hand. It tickled and Laura started to giggle.

"What are you doing here?" Laura asked the man curiously.

The man pointed to the collecting

tin he was holding. Written on it were the words 'Sunshine Circus'.

"Our circus always has to close in the winter because it is too cold for people to sit in a tent to watch the show. Usually we make enough money in the summer to pay for all the animal food until spring, but not many families want to come to the circus these days. Unfortunately we

haven't found anywhere to keep Polly yet either," the man said sadly. "She needs a nice meadow to gallop about in, and a warm stable to sleep in."

Laura looked at the pony. She really was very small indeed. Perhaps even small enough to fit into Laura's bedroom?

"Polly can live with us!" declared Laura.

The man laughed out loud.

"No, really!" Laura assured him. "My dad won't mind!"

The man shook his head. "I think I would need to talk to your dad about that," he said seriously.

Tommy tugged at Laura's arm. "Let's go!" he whispered.

"Please wait here!" Laura said to the man and she turned and raced off in the direction of home.

Tommy ran after her, puffing and panting. "We – were – meant – to – buy – some – bread!" he gasped.

But there was no time to buy bread now. Laura had to fetch Dad. And Dad could explain to the man that Polly could stay with them.

Laura has an Idea

Laura burst into the kitchen, Tommy panting behind her. Breathlessly, she explained about Polly. But Dad shook his head, just as the man from the circus had done.

"You can't possibly keep a pony in a flat!" he exclaimed.

Laura glared at him crossly.

"But you said that if a pony were small enough, it would fit into my bedroom and . . ."

Once again Dad shook his head.

"A pony needs a proper stable, Laura, and a field to run in. Imagine how bad the flat would smell if she left her droppings everywhere!" he explained. "It's just not possible."

Just then the door opened and Mum came in.

"Mum! I've met this little pony, and she doesn't have a home. Please say we can help her," Laura cried, bursting into tears.

"Whatever is all this?" said Mum, putting down her cello and giving Laura a big hug.

Laura was crying too much to talk, so Tommy and Dad told Mum all about the man with the pony.

"Oh Laura!" Mum said softly. "I'm afraid Dad is right. A pony needs a meadow and a stable. It wouldn't be at all happy living in a flat."

"But where else can Polly live?" sobbed Laura.

"I'm certain the man from the circus will find a home for her," said Dad.

Laura ran to her bedroom and slammed the door. She took her piggybank down from the shelf. If Polly couldn't live with them, then at least Laura would make sure there was enough money for her food. But when Laura had counted all her money she gave a huge sigh. She wouldn't be able to feed Polly for even a week!

Sadly Laura slumped on her bed. As she lay there, a sparkle of light caught her eye. She rolled over, and there was her special star tumbling around the room.

"Oh Star, I'm so glad you're here. What can I do to help poor Polly?" Laura sighed.

The star twinkled as it flitted from picture to picture on Laura's wall and stopped over a drawing Laura had made of a horse in Granny and Grandad's meadow.

"Of course, Star!" Laura cried.

"Granny and Grandad's meadow!
What a brilliant idea! There are
stables next door too. It will be
perfect for Polly!"

Laura jumped up and ran to
tell Mum, Dad and Tommy her
great idea.

"I'm not sure that it will be
possible, Laura," said Mum.

"Don't get your hopes up,
Laura," said Dad.

"Hurry, Laura! Call them up!" yelled Tommy excitedly.

It seemed to take ages for Granny to answer the phone. And then it took even longer before she was able to understand what Laura was saying.

Finally it was Granny's turn to speak. "I will have to discuss it first with Grandad. I'll call you back in half an hour, I promise!" she said.

The next half-hour passed very slowly indeed. Laura took the telephone everywhere with her. She was too anxious even to eat lunch. At last the telephone rang. Her heart thudding wildly, Laura grabbed the phone.

"Well, Laura," said Granny. "There's enough room for another pony in the stable next door. The man from the circus can bring Polly here this afternoon if he wants."

"Thank you, Granny!" Laura shrieked with happiness. "Mum, Dad! Can we go and tell the man from the circus now? Please, before he disappears."

A Home for Polly

Later that day, Laura and Tommy were sitting in front of Granny and Grandad's house, waiting for Polly to arrive.

Her owner, Mr Binnie, had been amazed when they had all run down to the corner and Dad had explained he had a home for Polly for the winter. Mr Binnie had been

so happy, and had thanked them
over and over again.

"Where is Polly? Why is it taking
them so long?" complained Tommy.

"Mr Binnie has to take Polly to
the trailer first and then drive really
slowly, so that she doesn't become
carsick," said Laura.

Tommy could understand that.

He sometimes felt carsick too!

Laura couldn't sit still any longer. She jumped up, hopping from foot to foot in excitement.

"I'm bored!" moaned Tommy. "I'm going to go and play."

But at that very moment a small circus van, with a trailer attached to it, drove around the corner.

The van was painted in lovely bright colours. On the roof was a chimney, so that it looked just like a proper house.

"Hurray, they're here!" Laura cheered and she ran towards the van to greet Polly. Tommy chased after her.

Mr Binnie parked the van in the

meadow next to the house. He then led the pony down the trailer-ramp. Laura gulped anxiously. Would Polly really be happy here?

Polly neighed. Mr Binnie gave her a pat and off she trotted across the meadow.

Her tail flew out behind her and her hooves moved so fast that Laura could hardly see them touch the grass.

"Well, she seems to like it here!" Mr Binnie said happily.

Laura wanted to stroke Polly, but she understood that the little pony needed some exercise after her journey. There would be plenty of time for them to spend together!

After a good gallop, Polly slowed down and trotted back to the van.

"Do you want to give her a brush?" asked Mr Binnie. "She loves it!"

Laura thought this was a super idea, but Tommy was a bit worried.

"Is it safe?" he asked Mr Binnie. "Horses can kick quite hard, can't they?"

"Polly only ever does that when she is afraid," replied Mr Binnie. He handed Laura a flat, round brush and showed her how to rub Polly down properly.

Tommy soon found the courage to stroke the pony and a big smile spread across his face.

"She's lovely!" he cried. He then helped Laura to groom Polly's coat, but he took care not to stand behind the pony, just in case it startled her.

Grooming was hard work, but Laura was enjoying herself so much she didn't want to stop, even when Granny called them in for supper.

Starry Night

That evening Laura and Tommy
stayed with Granny and Grandad.
Tommy was soon fast asleep, but
Laura kept thinking of Polly.
Tomorrow they would introduce her
to the other ponies, but tonight she
was alone in the meadow.

Laura was worried about how
Polly would feel being in a strange

place. Unable to lie in bed any longer, Laura finally got up. She put on her jacket and wellington boots and crept outside the house into the meadow.

How quiet it was! The only sounds she could hear were the whispering of the wind and the occasional noise of a car as it passed by in the distance. It was really quite spooky.

But then Laura heard Polly whinny softly.

She was awake too! Laura walked up to her and stroked her thick mane.

"Can't you sleep either, Polly?" asked Laura. "Are you lonely?"

Polly neighed again and rubbed her nose against the front of Laura's jacket.

"I know!" whispered Laura. "I'll introduce you to my special friend, the star. It will look after you and you won't be alone any longer."

Laura gazed up into the sky. There amongst all the other stars was her very own special star. It twinkled and sparkled, then slowly cartwheeled down to where Laura and Polly were standing, leaving a trail of sparkling stardust in its wake.

"This is Polly," Laura told her star. "And Polly, this is my star," she said to Polly. Polly stretched out her neck inquisitively.

The star did a somersault before very gently touching Polly with one of its points. It then spun off across the meadow to look at the brightly-coloured poles.

"They are for the gymkhana tomorrow," explained Laura. "The ponies have to jump over them."

The star tested the poles out by springing over them. Laura clapped her hands in delight. "You could take part in the gymkhana too, Star," she said.

Polly stepped towards the poles inquisitively, and suddenly Laura had the most wonderful thought. Of course – she could take part in the gymkhana now – she could ride Polly! She would ask Mr Binnie first thing in the morning!

Just then, Laura's star drifted towards them again. Laura took it into her arms and gave it a big hug.

"It's such a shame that you won't be there too!" she said.

The star drifted across to Polly

and touched the patch on Polly's
forehead with one of its points so
that it sparkled magically. In the
light of the moon Laura could see
that the patch looked just like a
little star.

"That will remind me of
you, Star!" sighed Laura happily.
Laura's star turned a huge
cartwheel across the meadow.
Polly neighed contentedly and
cantered off after it.

Laura yawned and realised

how tired she was. She could hardly keep her eyes open. "Goodnight!" she called out to Polly and her star, and turned back towards the house.

Before getting into bed she took one more look out of the window: Polly and her star were still playing.

"Polly won't be lonely any more," thought Laura happily to herself as she cuddled up in bed. "Oh, I do hope Mr Binnie says we can ride in the gymkhana tomorrow," she murmured sleepily.

The Gymkhana

The next morning Laura was awake long before the rest of the family. She quickly pulled on her clothes, crept out of the house and rushed across the meadow just as Mr Binnie appeared.

"Hello, Laura," he said. "You are up bright and early! You are just in time to help me feed Polly."

"Great!" said Laura. "Actually, Mr Binnie, I have a big favour to ask you," she added quickly before her courage failed her.

When Laura told him about her plan, Mr Binnie was hesitant.

"Polly has never taken part in a gymkhana before," he said. "I am

sure she could do simple things like walking round the ring, she is used to that. But I don't know about going over jumps."

Laura wasn't worried. She was sure everything would go to plan. Then Mr Binnie said, "And have you asked your parents yet? What do they think?"

"I will ask them, Mr Binnie, as soon as they are up, but I am sure they will say yes," she said. And as soon as she had finished feeding Polly, Laura ran back to the house.

Granny and Grandad were making breakfast, and Tommy was sitting at the kitchen table drinking a glass of milk.

"Mr Binnie says I can ride Polly in the gymkhana today, Granny," Laura said. "I would love that so much. Please may I?"

"Well that decision is up to Mum and Dad," said Granny.

"Do you have all the proper equipment, Laura?" asked Grandad. "You can't ride a pony without a proper hat and boots."

Dad came into the kitchen looking a bit sleepy.

"Please may I ride Polly in the gymkhana, Dad?" asked Laura. "I could wear my wellington boots and my cycle helmet, so I would be safe. It would be so exciting. Please, Dad!"

"We would need to ask Mr Binnie about that first," Dad replied.

"I have!" smiled Laura. "He has already said yes."

"Oh Laura," Dad laughed. "If your mum agrees, then yes, I think it would be all right."

"Hurray!" shouted Laura and raced off to find Mum. Mum helped Laura to get ready, and before long it was time for the gymkhana to start.

* * *

Crowds of people had gathered in the meadow. There were lots of children with their ponies and their families who had come to watch.

Mum, Dad, Tommy, Granny and Grandad all smiled at Laura

from the front row. Her heart was beating wildly as Mr Binnie lifted her up on to Polly's back. She felt excited and anxious all at the same time. She was finally riding Polly!

Laura tried hard to sit upright just like she had learned to do in her riding lessons. From up high on

Polly's back it seemed a long way down to the ground!

Mr Binnie led Polly to the line of ponies. Polly stood there and looked around curiously.

"Walk on!" called out Laura and she squeezed the pony's fat tummy with her legs. This is what she had learned to do at riding school, to make the pony move forwards.

Polly started to walk forwards towards a group of brightly-coloured poles. There was lots of bustle in the ring with ponies and people everywhere.

Laura bounced a bit from side to side, but otherwise everything

was fine. She even managed to
wave at her family, all lined up by
the side of the ring. They waved
back and cheered, though Mum
looked rather anxious. Laura felt
very proud. She was actually taking
part in a real gymkhana!

Everyone in the audience started

to clap. But oh dear, what was happening? The applause seemed to remind Polly of the circus. All of a sudden she threw her head up towards the sky, gave a loud neigh and started to turn in a circle as if she wanted to dance.

Laura gripped Polly tightly with her knees and said again, "Walk on, Polly." She tried to steer the excited pony into the line with all the other ponies.

Laura suddenly felt very anxious. Polly had no intention of getting into line. Instead she kicked out her hind legs and sat down!

Laura desperately clung on to Polly's mane. "Don't do that!" she

shouted. "I'm falling off!" But Polly
didn't listen.

"Get up!" exclaimed Laura.
All the other ponies were queuing
behind Polly. Laura was feeling
very hot and bothered.

Polly got back up on to her feet
again and started to trot in a circle.
Laura was concentrating so hard on

staying on that she quite forgot to sit up straight. She continued to cling tightly on to Polly's mane.

Laura was starting to feel really rather annoyed with Polly. This wasn't meant to happen! The entire audience was laughing at her!

Then, the worst thing of all happened. Polly bent her forelegs, knelt down and lowered her head to

the ground. It was as if she was trying to bow!

Laura squeezed her legs around Polly's middle but slowly and surely she slipped down the pony's back. And then, thump! Laura fell on to the grass. She didn't hurt herself, but she felt this was quite the worst thing that had ever happened to her in her whole life.

Her face a deep shade of pink, Laura jumped up and ran from the gymkhana ring as fast as her legs could carry her.

A Very Special Pony

Laura found a quiet spot where she could be on her own. She could still hear the audience laughing and she felt so ashamed. Polly had made such a fool of her! Laura felt she would never, ever ride a pony again.

"Oh Star! What on earth shall I do now?" asked Laura despairingly.

Just then, Mr Binnie walked

around the corner with Mum, Dad and Tommy. "Why, whatever is wrong, Laura?" he asked.

"Everyone is laughing at me! It's all Polly's fault," Laura wailed.

"Oh no, Laura!" said Dad, giving her a big hug. "Everyone loved you and Polly!"

"Come on," Mr Binnie said, "let's go and have a nice cup of tea," and he led everyone off towards his van.

They all squeezed in and looked around in astonishment. There was a comfy sofa and a table, and even an oven and a sink. It was like a complete home in miniature!

On the walls were pictures from the circus of tightrope walkers, clowns and ponies, including Polly! She was wearing a headdress with a plumed feather on top.

"You see, Laura, you mustn't be upset with Polly. She was only doing what she was used to in the circus," said Mr Binnie. "It is a wonderful thing to make people laugh. Not many people can do that."

Laura looked at the picture of Polly performing in the circus ring.

She'd only been doing the things she knew made people happy, and Laura had been so cross with her. Poor Polly! Laura felt terrible.

"Here, Laura," said Mr Binnie, handing Laura Polly's feather headdress. "Polly loves wearing this. You could both do one last turn in the ring. Everyone would love it."

Laura, Tommy and Mr Binnie went out to Polly, and Mr Binnie fixed the headdress to her halter. Polly nodded her head so that the feather-plume swayed to and fro.

Laura's attention was drawn to the patch on the pony's forehead. It glittered and sparkled brightly with stardust.

"I am really sorry, Polly," whispered Laura. "I didn't realise just how special you are."

Mr Binnie then helped Laura up on to Polly's back.

Laura didn't mind going back out in front of the audience now. In fact, Laura felt rather proud sitting high up on Polly's back.

Laura did another lap of the gymkhana ring. This time she realised that people were not laughing at her, but because they loved Polly. And Laura loved her too.

That evening, before Laura, Tommy and their parents drove back home, Laura ran to see Polly one last time to say goodbye.

"I'll come back again soon!" she assured Polly. "Mr Binnie says I can ride you every weekend so we can learn to do gymkhana together."

Just then Laura looked up at the sky. There among the stars was her special friend. "Take care of Polly for me!" whispered Laura to her star and she waved up at it.

Laura's star turned a giant cartwheel in the sky and left a trail of sparkling stardust as it went. And, with a beam of starlight, it waved back at Laura.